THE
MAGIC FEATHER

Grateful acknowledgment is made to Walter Jekyll and his excellent collection, *Jamaica Song and Story*, published for the English Folklore Society, London, 1907. Big thanks are due to Handel Whitmore and Kristin Harpster, whose expertise lent this retelling authenticity. We also wish to thank all the folklorists whose versions of the bird of darkness and other Anancy stories are available for readers everywhere.   —L.R.

Library of Congress Cataloging-in-Publication Data

Rojany, Lisa.
The magic feather: a Jamaican legend / retold by Lisa Rojany ; illustrated by Philip Kuznicki.
p.   cm.—(Legends of the world)
Summary: Solidae must pull a feather from the dreaded Mancrow to bring color and light back to the island of Jamaica.
ISBN 0-8167-3751-7 (lib.)   ISBN 0-8167-3752-5 (pbk.)
[1. Folklore--Jamaica.]   I. Kuznicki, Philip, ill.   II. Title.
III. Series.
PZ8.1.R66Mag   1995   [398.2]—dc20   95-9982

THE
MAGIC FEATHER

A JAMAICAN LEGEND

RETOLD BY LISA ROJANY   ILLUSTRATED BY PHILIP KUZNICKI

TROLL ASSOCIATES

ong ago, when humans an' animals could speak as brothers and sisters, a girl named Solidae lived on the island of Jamaica with her old gran'mother. Havin' grown up in the forest, Solidae was strong and quick. Nimble as a coney, she scampered up trees. Every day Solidae went into the forest to gather breadfruit, papaw, coconut, an' mango, or she used her gran'mother's net to catch colorful fish.

But one day Solidae came to her gran'mother, puzzled and angry.

"Gran'mother," she said, hangin' the empty net on the wall. "The fish used to shine like rainbows in the water. Now they are the color of mud. What is wrong?"

With her gray head bent low, her gran'mother sighed. "The colors are goin' away. That must mean Mancrow is back."

"Mancrow?" Solidae asked.

Her gran'mother made a large circle in the air with her hands. "A long time ago strange creatures roamed the earth. Some had the bodies of animals but spoke as humans. Some had the bodies of humans but the hearts of beasts. Only one creature had all of these. He was the Mancrow."

Solidae leaned forward, listenin' hard.

"Mancrow's body was half human, half beautifully feathered bird. He spoke as a human, but his heart was dark as a savage beast's. Time passed an' the creatures changed. Animals became all animal, an' humans became all human. Only Mancrow refused to be either. He went alone to the dark reaches of the forest. With no one to admire him, all but one of his colorful feathers turned black. That's when he started to make trouble."

Gran'mother's eyes were worried as she looked up at Solidae. "I must go to the village for a few days. I will be back as soon as I can. Be careful in the forest, dawta of my heart. Stay far from the Mancrow. If you see him, run away. Do not speak to him, les' you anger him."

"I'll be careful, Gran'mother," was all that Solidae said. She took up her *bankra,* or basket, and went out to pick mangoes.

In the middle of the forest, she met up with her friend, Iguana. Solidae chased Iguana up a mango tree, her strong fingers an' toes findin' niches to climb.

"Is the fruit ripe, Iguana?" she called.

There was no answer. Where had Iguana gone? Solidae looked in all the dark holes, then behind the thick brown branches an' broad green leaves.

Finally she heard, "Solidae! I'm out here-here-here!"

She pushed aside broad green leaves an' saw Iguana next to a cluster of ripe fruit. As Iguana hissed with glee, rubbin' his blue belly with both claws, he let go of the branch.

"Careful!" Solidae yelled.

But she was too late. Iguana teetered, then tumbled over and fell to the ground.

Before Solidae could move, a raspy voice screeched through the branches of the tree.

"You clumsy creature! Do you think because your skin has so many colors you can do as you please?"

Solidae craned her neck aroun' a shiny broad leaf. There was a man standin' over her friend, his arms spread wide.

No. Not arms, but wings! Black wings like a huge crow! Mancrow!

"It was an accident," Solidae yelled, forgetting her gran'mother's warnin' not to talk to Mancrow. "Don't hurt my friend! It was my fault he fell."

The crow raised his head an' squawked with fury.

"Who said that?" he demanded.

"Hush-hush-hush." Forgotten, Iguana darted away an' raced back up the tree. "Hush-hush-hush!"

Solidae looked to make sure her friend was all right, then stared at him in amazement. She knew this was Iguana, yet he looked so different! Gone were the shiny greens, the brilliant white, and the iridescent blues that warmed his silky skin. His body was now the color of mud. Even his shiny black eyes had faded to gray.

"What happened to you?"

"I do-do-do not know," said Iguana softly, touchin' his dull skin in misery.

Solidae thrust out her jaw an' pushed aside the leaves.

"You have done this!" she shouted down at Mancrow. "Give him back his colors!"

Iguana shook her leg.

"Do not look-look-look into his eyes," he whispered. "When I did I could not move-move-move!"

"Don't listen to that silly creature," crooned Mancrow. He peered up into the tree, red eyes glintin' beside his long, sharp beak. "Look at me an' you will see true beauty. I am so fine that you will admire me as all creatures should."

"I've seen enough of you," said Solidae, careful not to look at the crow's eyes. "If you won't give Iguana back his colors, then I think you're ugly an' horrible. I only wish you'd go away."

"Oh, I will go away," Mancrow screeched with rage. "But I will make sure that you never forget me!"

He spread his black wings wide an' began to spin in circles, faster an' faster. Lightnin' flashed an' the sky grew darker an' darker till all light vanished.

Solidae hugged Iguana, her heart beatin' wildly as thunder shook the tree. In the gloom aroun' her she could see only shadows an' shapes.

"Darkness there be an' darkness will remain," gloated the crow. "All color will be mine!"

As he spoke he wrapped his wings aroun' his body. Then he stepped away into the undergrowth, quickly vanishin' in the gloom.

"I think he's gone," Solidae finally whispered.

"It's so dark-dark-dark," Iguana mourned softly.

They felt their way down the tree an' out of the forest in silence. Solidae breathed deeply so she would not cry.

At the edge of the forest she spoke. "This is all my fault. Gran'mother warned me to be careful of the Mancrow. I am so sorry about your beautiful colors, an' about the darkness."

"Not your fault," Iguana said, then he looked up. "Perhaps you can ask your gran'mother for help-help-help. Maybe she knows what to do."

After the two friends said good-bye, Solidae made her way to the fern hut she shared with her gran'mother.

Days passed with no light to separate them from long, black nights. Because of the darkness, Solidae could not go into the forest to gather food. The leaves an' the trees drooped more each day. It was hard to see the forest she loved dying from lack of light. Harder still to know it was all her fault.

Finally her gran'mother came home, exhausted after her long walk from the village. Solidae helped put away her few bundles. She made a weak fire and steeped leaves for tea. As her gran'mother sipped the hot tea, Solidae told her all that had happened.

When she finished, her gran'mother let out a deep sigh an' nodded her head. "So that is where the great darkness come from."

"What does Mancrow do with all the colors?" Solidae asked.

"His colorful feather holds his power. He steals to keep his feather bright. Only if someone plucks that feather will the darkness end."

Solidae stood, "I will find Mancrow an' take his feather."

Her gran'mother shook her head but didn't argue. "I am too old and too tired to be much help to you. Be careful. Do not look into Mancrow's eyes, for they can freeze you. Do not let him raise his wings above your head, for he will steal your courage as he steals the color from your eyes."

Solidae nodded, her mind racin' with ideas. Her gran'mother prepared bulla cakes for the journey. Solidae packed other things she thought she might need an' she wrapped them with the cakes in a large bundle. Takin' her fishin' net from the wall, she turned an' gave her gran'mother a hug, then set off into the dark forest.

Solidae found trees an' climbed them, searchin' for a tree built the way she needed. Finally she found one. Not too big, not too t'ick, not too short, but just right. She tucked the net into a hollow spot an' set out the bulla cakes on a nearby limb.

Then she pulled an orchid from her bundle, its petals the brightest color she could find, an' tucked it in her hair.

She began to sing, scared that Mancrow would come an' scared that he wouldn't.

"Mancrow half human,
Mancrow half beast,
Come up to my tree
And share in my feast."

Three times she sang the song. The third time he was there, black wings beatin' at the foot of her tree.

"How dare you bring color into my forest!" Mancrow screeched.

Solidae gasped as if she had made a terrible mistake. She pulled the orchid from her hair an' replaced it with a flower the dull gray color of mud.

"Much better," said Mancrow.

"Why have you come, human?"

"To thank you for the darkness an' praise your beauty." Careful not to look in his eyes, Solidae gestured to the cakes an' sang,

"Mancrow half human,
Mancrow half beast,
Come up to my tree
And share in my feast."

Mancrow crowed with delight. "Finally, a smart human! Very well, you may give me your cakes."

"Oh, great Mancrow," said Solidae, "would you fly up here an' get one? I would love to see you fly. It would be a small thing for you to do for my delicious cakes."

Mancrow spread his wings an' the breeze ruffled his feathers.

"How shiny your wings are, an' how strong," said Solidae.

With a mighty jump, Mancrow swept into the air in front of her, his wings beatin' furiously.

"See," he crowed. "See how beautiful I am."

He tried to land next to her, but the branch was too small an' thin for his weight. He turned an' huge leaves tangled his wings, throwin' him off balance. As he teetered, Solidae grabbed her net an' threw it over him, then yanked it tight.

Mancrow tumbled to the forest floor. Putta-putta, cakes an' feathers flew everywhere. The more he struggled, the more tangled he became.

Solidae jumped to the ground an' threw herself on Mancrow, tryin' to hold him down. But even tied up, he was too strong for her.

She heard the sound of the net tearin'. Mancrow was usin' his talons to rip holes in the net! Soon he would escape!

"Help!" she cried out. "Help me, or he will get loose!"

From all about the forest, the animals came. A crocodile threw his body across Mancrow's legs, pinnin' him down. Birds, coneys, mongooses, frogs, an' lizards all helped to hold him tight. Iguana sat on Mancrow's beak an' hissed angrily in his face.

Her fingers shakin', Solidae ruffled through Mancrow's feathers. Hidden away beneath layers an' layers of black, she found the colorful tail feather an' yanked it out.

As she held up the feather for all to see, the island was filled with the first mornin' light in many days. Within and beyond the forest a roar of happiness sounded. People ran out of their homes an' danced in celebration. Colorful animals played in the light, an' sun-starved trees lifted their leaves skyward.

Solidae gathered up her torn net, an' Mancrow scurried off to hide.

"Thank you," Solidae said to her animal friends. "Without your help Mancrow would have escaped. I would never have gotten the feather."

Many years have passed, an' Solidae has kept that feather safe. As for Mancrow, she has not seen him yet. But when storms sweep across the island of Jamaica, Solidae keeps one eye on the sky an' asks everyone she knows, if the time come again, to help her bring the sun's light back. For after all these years, she worries that one day Mancrow's magic feather will grow in again.

The Caribbean Islands

Jamaica is a tropical island of rain forests and beaches, wide plains, sandy areas where cacti abound, and even stunted-tree forests on Blue Mountain, its highest peak. The island supports more than 200 species of birds, including Jamaica's national bird, the streamertail hummingbird. The story of Mancrow—half-man, half-crow—is a tale of West African origin, most likely brought to the island by African slaves.

Jamaica, which means "island of springs," was first inhabited by Arawak Indians. In 1494 Christopher Columbus claimed the island for Spain. The Spanish used Jamaica as a supply base and brought over men and women from West Africa to serve as slaves. For more than 300 years, until they were freed in 1838, the slaves toiled on the rich land. Today, the culture, beliefs, legends, and the art of the African people survive on the island along with the influences of the Spanish, British, and other Europeans. In fact, Jamaica's national motto, *Out of Many, One People*, describes a society of many races.